To the students
of St. Room 9
And ~
Imagine all
you can do
and be!
Sandy Philipson
'×01

RS Takatsu
'×01

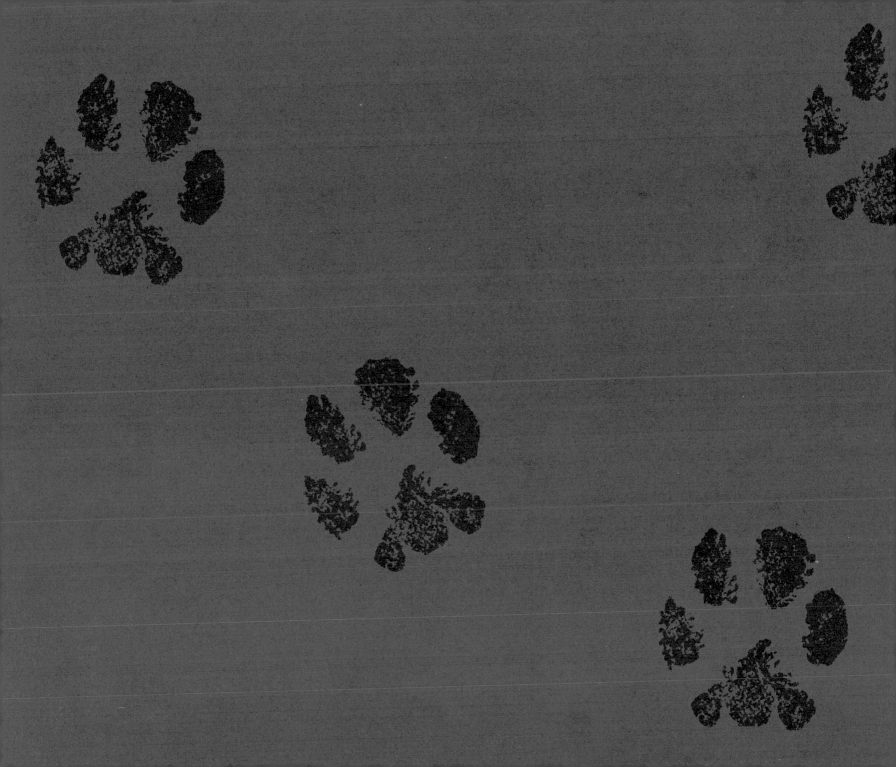

MAX & Annie

this Book belongs to:

_____

_____

_____

This book is dedicated to Bob whose talent and teachings
have opened the door to many imaginations.

A company where children have a voice.

www.voiceofkids.com

Chagrin River Publishing Company
P.O. Box 173
Chagrin Falls, Ohio 44022
(440) 893-9250

First Edition
Printed in the United States of America
10 9 8 7 6 5 4 3 2 1

Library of Congress Catalog Card Number 00-108582
Philipson, Sandra.
The Artist / by Sandra Philipson; illustrated by Robert Takatch
Summary: Max and Annie learn about the power of imagination from a magical artist.
ISBN 1-929821-03-4 (hardcover)
[1. Adventure story—Juvenile Fiction. 2. Picture book—Juvenile Fiction.
3. English Springer Spaniels—Juvenile Fiction. 4. Friendship—Juvenile Fiction.
5. Dog story for Children. 6. Art book for children—Juvenile Fiction.]

The Artist

A Max and Annie Adventure in Imagination

written by
Sandra J. Philipson

illustrated by
Robert Takatch

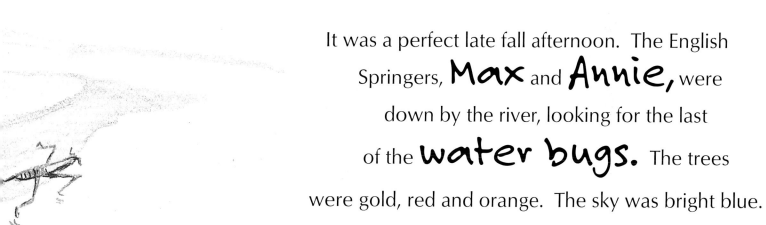

It was a perfect late fall afternoon. The English Springers, **Max** and **Annie,** were down by the river, looking for the last of the **water bugs.** The trees were gold, red and orange. The sky was bright blue.

Suddenly, Max thought he saw something move on the other side of the river. There was a flash of white and a soft rustling in the brush on the top of the river bank.

Max and Annie decided to investigate.

They swam across the river and scrambled up the steep bank. Max was the first one up. Annie was a little slower since she had lost her front leg to cancer earlier that year. Still, even with three legs, she kept up pretty well. Max looked around while he waited for Annie to finish climbing.

Over in the tall grass sat a man holding a large white paper. He was a big man sitting on a small canvas chair. He wore a Western hat on his head, a dark blue denim shirt, jeans, boots, and he had a big white beard. His eyes twinkled when he saw Max and Annie.

"Ssh!" he said **"You two will scare the birds."**

"What birds?" demanded Max. "I'm the best bird chaser in the whole valley, **bring em on!"** boasted Max.

Max and Annie looked around, but neither of them saw any birds. They ventured closer to the old man and saw that he was holding a large piece of drawing paper and a red pastel pencil. He was drawing quickly, and when he was finished, the paper started to move. Max and Annie watched in amazement as a pair of cardinals on the paper began to cock their heads and stretch their wings. Then, in a split second, the **birds burst from the paper,** took off into the air, circled the dogs as if to say goodbye, and flew off down the river. The dogs were astounded and scared. Max hid his head in the bushes. Annie was wide eyed, but the old artist spoke softly to them.

"Don't be frightened you two. Come over here and look at the picture I just drew."

Annie nudged Max's backside, and he lifted his head out of the bushes. Now Max's **curiosity** was stronger than his fear. He and Annie moved in a little closer. They could see a picture of the sparkling river, and that was tempting for Max. The artist spoke to the dog.

"I bet a young dog like you would love to jump from the cliff over there, sail through the air, and land in the river as softly as a Canada Goose."

Max edged even closer, staring at the paper. Before he could blink, he was running at top speed toward the river. Without any hesitation, he threw himself over the cliff edge. Max felt himself flying in the air, but somehow he wasn't afraid. He was excited to be in the air. After a minute, he hit the water, back feet first and with a soft **splash** came down in the river. It was a perfect landing. He laughed and rolled over in the water, delighted to be in the river. Max closed his eyes while he **paddled and played** in the cool water. When he opened his eyes again, he was at the feet of the artist, staring at the picture of the river. The water twinkled in the sunlight. He stood up to shake off but found that **he wasn't wet.**

Annie was beginning to realize that **this wasn't an ordinary picture or artist.**

"Do you want to try a dream too, girl?" asked the man gently. Annie looked thoughtful; she was always more cautious than Max, but this was too wonderful not to try. She nodded.

"Come here then." he said to Annie.

She nudged the dazed Max out of the way and looked into the picture. The artist patted her head and began to draw.

Annie looked down. She had all four legs again, and she was running across a field of tall grass. She sprung up easily over a fallen tree with room to spare and chased a squirrel for what seemed an eternity. She was panting but didn't feel the least bit tired. Her legs felt like springs in the air; **she could run like this forever.** Annie was free of anything that weighed her down.

She yelped in delight, rolled over on her back, and found herself being **scratched behind the ears** by the old artist.

"How was that memory, girl? Nice?" he asked.

Annie sighed contentedly. Whether she had three legs or four, both Annie and the artist knew that it was her **spirit** that made her whole.

"Let's see, **how about one for me?"** the man said to himself and his visitors.

Max and Annie looked at the paper expectantly. The picture darkened to a moonlit field. The autumn leaves were falling like confetti in the breeze. A **young couple** walked together under the stars. They were carrying canvases, papers and easels. The young woman was slim with brown hair that curled around her face. The man was tall and strong.

In the middle of the field they both stopped, put down the easels they had been carrying and danced together in the moonlight. It was a moment of years ago or yet another lifetime.

The artist smiled as the paper lightened.

"**Memories, adventures,** and **dreams** are gifts of magic we can all create for ourselves. Pictures you draw and words you write can come alive if you open yourself to your imagination."

Then he laughed and continued, "I must have some imagination, **talking to dogs . . .**"

As Max and Annie got up to go home, they glanced again at the white paper. To their astonishment, the picture on the sheet was not one of the river, or of birds, or young couples. It was a picture of their dog house, and they were standing in front of it waiting for their supper.

"This will get you home quicker than you can run. **Now off with you both,"** laughed the artist.

Max and Annie took off down the river bank just as the autumn sun was setting. When they turned to look back, the old man waved as he packed up his papers and pastel pencils.

In the blink of an eye, they were home having dinner and getting ready to dream their own dreams for the night.

Before they went to sleep, Max asked Annie, "Do you think we will ever see the artist again?" "Whenever we want to, Max," she replied. "Now close your eyes and **think, imagine, remember . . . sweet dreams.**"

The Real Max and Annie

**Max and Annie are
English Springer Spaniels who
live in Chagrin Falls, Ohio.**

Max is three years old, or twenty-one in dog years. Max was a terrible terror of a puppy. He chewed pants and pillows; he dug holes and chased moles, and he never came when he was called unless he was real hungry. He was hit by a pick-up truck, lost in the woods in a snow storm, rescued when he fell through the ice in a swamp, pecked on by a gaggle of geese, and almost caught in quick sand. He is lucky to be alive!

Annie thinks he is a pain most of the time, but sometimes he has a good idea, like raiding the trash or picking the roasted chicken off the kitchen counter. She likes it too because he always gets blamed.

Annie is Max's dog big sister. She is ten years old or seventy in dog years. She has always been well-behaved, well-bred, and well-trained. She was almost the perfect puppy. When she was twelve weeks old she chewed a tiny hole in the arm of the new leather chair, and later that week she spilled a whole bottle of pancake syrup on the kitchen floor. That was nine years ago; she hasn't done anything naughty since!

We know she loves Max because they sometimes "talk" to each other and kiss when she is in the mood. Annie is the boss of Max, but he doesn't care because all he wants to do is hunt, chase, run, swim, eat, and get lovies from the family.

In December, 1998, Annie had her left front leg removed because she had cancer. She's a little slower now, but she still enjoys a run in the woods.

Read more about Max and Annie. There are two other books in the series: <u>Annie Loses Her Leg but Finds Her Way</u> and <u>Max's Wild Goose Chase</u>.

Visit both dogs and order books on our web site *maxandannie.com*.

Let's write!

The artist takes Max and Annie on a journey through their imaginations. Where would you like the artist to take you? What would you like to do when you get there?

Let's draw!

Create a picture of where you would like the magical artist to take you.